·ADDY·

THE BOOKS ABOUT ADDY

MEET ADDY • An American Girl
Addy and her mother try to escape from slavery because
they hope to be free and to reunite their family.

ADDY LEARNS A LESSON • A School Story
Addy starts her life as a free person in Philadelphia.
She learns about reading and writing—and freedom.

ADDY'S SURPRISE • A Christmas Story
Addy and Momma are generous with the little money
they've saved—and thrilled by a great surprise.

HAPPY BIRTHDAY, ADDY! • A Springtime Story
Addy makes a new friend, who encourages her to
claim a birthday and helps her face prejudice.

ADDY SAVES THE DAY • A Summer Story
The Civil War is over, but not the feud between Addy and
Harriet, until tragedy forces them to come together at last.

CHANGES FOR ADDY • A Winter Story
The long struggle to reunite Addy's family finally ends,
but there is heartache along with the happiness.

◆

WELCOME TO ADDY'S WORLD • 1864
American history is lavishly illustrated
with photographs, illustrations, and
excerpts from real girls' letters and diaries.

1864
MEET
ADDY
An American Girl

BY CONNIE PORTER

ILLUSTRATIONS DAHL TAYLOR, MELODYE ROSALES

VIGNETTES RENÉE GRAEF, LUANN ROBERTS

American Girl

SCHOLASTIC INC.

New York Toronto London Auckland Sydney
Mexico City New Delhi Hong Kong Buenos Aires

PICTURE CREDITS
The following individuals and organizations have generously given permission to reprint
illustrations contained in "Looking Back": pp. 62-63—Massachusetts Commandery Military
Order of the Loyal Legion and the U.S. Army Military History Institute (slave family in
wagon); Courtesy Library of Congress (Phillis Wheatley); Maryland Historical Society,
Baltimore (Benjamin Banneker); Courtesy Library of Congress (captive Africans); Courtesy of
the Witte Museum and the San Antonio Museum Association, San Antonio, Texas (cabinet);
Missouri Historical Society Por-H-4 (slave nurse); Photographs and Prints Division,
Schomburg Center for Research in Black Culture, The New York Public Library, Astor, Lenox,
and Tilden Foundations (slaves in field); pp. 64-65—Chicago Historical Society x1354 (leg
irons); New York Historical Society (slave cabins); Courtesy Library of Congress (slave
family); The Stagville Center of the North Carolina Division of Archives and History (slave
doll); pp. 66-67—North Carolina Division of Archives and History (slave gathering);
Smithsonian Institution Photo No. 81-11790 (gourd fiddle); Culver Pictures (Nat Turner);
Chicago Historical Society ICHi-06599 (advertisement); North Wind Picture Archives (slave
auction); pp. 68-69—Eastman Johnson (1824-1906), *A Ride for Liberty—The Fugitive Slaves*, c.
1862. Gift of Miss Gwendolyn O.L. Conkling, The Brooklyn Museum; Courtesy Library of
Congress (Harriet Tubman); The National Portrait Gallery, Smithsonian Institution Photo No.
NPG.74.75 (Frederick Douglass); Courtesy Friends Historical Library, Swarthmore College
(Henry "Box" Brown); Bettman Archive (battle scene).

Edited by Roberta Johnson
Designed by Myland McRevey and Jane S. Varda
Art Directed by Kathleen A. Brown and Jane S. Varda
Cover Background by Dahl Taylor

ISBN 0-439-39064-8

12 11 10 9 8 7 6 5 4 3 2 1   2 3 4 5 6 7/0

Printed in the U.S.A.   23

First Scholastic printing, February 2002

TO MY GRANDMOTHERS,
ADELLE HOUSTON AND
MARY JEMISON DUNN,
FOR THE WAY BACK TO MY ADDY

TABLE OF CONTENTS

ADDY'S FAMILY
AND FRIENDS

CHAPTER ONE
WHISPERS OF FREEDOM   1

CHAPTER TWO
SOLD!   10

CHAPTER THREE
A NEW PLAN   22

CHAPTER FOUR
INTO THE NIGHT   33

CHAPTER FIVE
FREEDOM TAKEN   48

LOOKING BACK   61

ADDY'S FAMILY

POPPA
Addy's father, whose dream gives the family strength.

MOMMA
Addy's mother, whose love helps the family survive.

ADDY
A courageous girl, smart and strong, growing up during the Civil War.

SAM
Addy's fifteen-year-old brother, determined to be free.

ESTHER
Addy's one-year-old sister.

MASTER STEVENS
*The man who owns
Addy and her family.*

AUNTIE LULA
*The cook on the
plantation who looks
out for Addy's family.*

UNCLE SOLOMON
*Auntie Lula's husband,
who gives good advice.*

MISS CAROLINE
*A woman who helps
Momma and Addy.*

WHISPERS OF
FREEDOM

Addy Walker woke up late on a
summer's night to hear her parents
whispering. She thought no more of
their quiet voices than of the soft chirping of the
crickets in the woods just beyond the little cabin.
Often she awoke to her parents' whispering. Addy
liked the sound. It made her feel safe, knowing her
mother and father were close by.

A small fire glowed in the hearth as the last
coals burned down from the fire Momma had
used to cook supper. Usually Addy liked the
warm glow of the coals in the darkness. It was
the only light in the windowless cabin. But tonight
it just made her hotter. Sweat crawled down her

small body like ants. The stiff, dry cornhusks stuffing her pallet poked through their thin covering, sticking her. Her older brother Sam lay on his own pallet near her feet. Addy could see his dark face in the firelight and hear his regular breathing. Her baby sister Esther lay next to her. Esther's steamy breath was blowing on Addy's face. Addy loved Esther, but it was too hot to be close to her tonight. Addy tried to wiggle away from the baby. When she turned from Esther, her parents stopped talking.

"Hush, Ben," Momma said to Poppa. "I think Addy woke up."

Addy kept her eyes closed, but she could hear the rustle of cornhusks when her father got up. His feet softly crossed the dirt floor. She opened her eyes just slightly as his shadow passed over her, covering her and Esther and Sam. Addy felt protected inside of it. She wanted to ask, "Poppa, what you and Momma talking about?" But she kept her mouth shut. When her parents started talking again, she listened.

"That child asleep, Ruth," Poppa said to Momma, returning to their pallet. "She tired out.

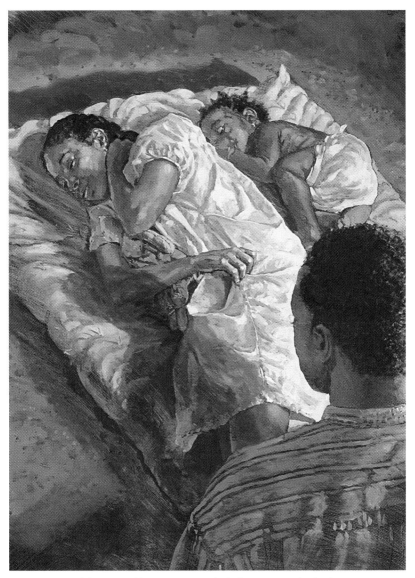

Addy opened her eyes just slightly as Poppa's shadow
passed over her. She felt protected inside it.

They had the children out in the fields half the day worming the tobacco plants."

"Ben, listen to me," Momma said. Her voice was serious. "I don't think we should run now. The war is gonna be over soon, and then we'll be free."

"Ruth, I've done told you before, them Union soldiers ain't nowhere near our part of North Carolina. They all the way clear on the other side of the state," Addy's father replied. "Who knows when we gonna be free?"

"But Ben, we can't lose nothing by waiting. We all together here. That count for something," Momma argued.

"Ruth, it should count, but you know it don't. With this war, times hard. Money is real tight for the masters. A whole group of slaves was sold off the Gifford plantation because Master Gifford couldn't afford to feed and clothe them," Poppa said.

"That was Master Gifford. Master Stevens would never sell us. We work hard for him. We do everything he tell us. He need me to do sewing, and you do his carpenter work." Addy had never heard her mother speak so firmly.

"What about Sam?" Poppa went on. "I got to drag him off his pallet when the morning work horn sound. He get up grumbling about not wanting to work for the master, and he take his grumbling out into the fields. He got a hot head and a hot mouth. Sam done run off once, and now he want to go fight in the war. All he talk about is going north to fight for freedom. If Sam don't watch it, he gonna be getting us all in trouble."

Addy didn't like what she heard. She remembered when Sam had run off the year before, shortly before Esther was born. He was tracked down by Master Stevens's dogs and brought back. He was tied to a tree and beaten with a whip by Master Stevens. Addy screamed and cried, but her parents did not. They had blank, empty faces that made Addy angry. When the beating was over, Sam's back was covered with blood. Poppa carried him back to the cabin, and Momma and Poppa cleaned the blood from him. Finally Addy yelled at her parents, "Y'all don't care about Sam at all! Y'all not even crying." As soon as she said it, she felt bad.

whip

"Come here," her father had said softly. Addy went to him, ashamed to look at his dark, stubbly face. She held her face down, but her father lifted it and wiped away her tears. "Just because you don't see us crying and carrying on don't mean we don't care. It don't mean we ain't crying, either. Me and your momma crying on the inside. We ain't always free to show our feelings on the outside. But on the inside we is free. There's always freedom inside your head, Addy."

Freedom. That was what her parents were talking about tonight. But they were talking about a different kind of freedom. They were talking about the kind of freedom a slave had to run away to get.

"If Sam take off by himself a second time, we might never see him again," Momma said in a worried whisper. "I want us all to be together."

Poppa didn't answer right away. Then he said, "Uncle Solomon told me in the field today that there's a set of railroad tracks about ten miles after the river near the Gifford place. We follow them north till they cross another set of tracks. Where they cross, there's a white house with red shutters. It's a safe house. An old white woman live there,

named Miss Caroline. She gonna help us. We
only got to get that far," Poppa said.

In the dark, Addy hugged Janie, the small
rag doll Momma had made for her, the doll
she slept with every night. Her parents'
talk about running away scared her. She
had never heard them talk about it before.
Whenever Sam talked about escaping, they
told him to hush up.

"If we get caught, Master Stevens gonna split
us up for sure," Momma said, her voice shaky.

"I figure ain't nothing for sure," answered
Poppa, "but we got to take our chances while we
got 'em. You can't go backing out on me now."

"I'm not backing out," Momma said. She
sounded cross. "I'm just scared. You want to go
all the way to Philadelphia. I ain't never been no
farther than the Gifford plantation. What if we get
lost from each other?"

"We gonna go together and we gonna stay
together. God will watch over us. You got to
believe we gonna make it north." Poppa sounded
sure and strong. Addy knew he could protect them,
no matter what.

"Let's just wait a little longer. When the war over, we all gonna be free. All of us right here," Momma said again.

But Poppa was firm. "I hurt when I see Addy toting heavy water buckets to the fields, or when I see her working there, bent over like a old woman. Sam already fifteen, but she a little girl, nine years old, and smart as they come. She go out in the morning, her eyes all bright and shining with hope. By night she come stumbling in here so tired, she can hardly eat. Esther still a little baby, but Addy getting beat down every day. I can't stand back and watch it no more. We can't wait for our freedom. We gonna have to take it."

Momma was quiet again. Addy wasn't thinking about the heat of the cabin, her prickly pallet, or Esther's hot breath. She was waiting for her mother's answer. None came. She heard her father rise. He went to the hearth and covered the coals with ashes.

When Addy heard him lie down, her eyes popped open, but now Addy could see nothing. There was no light in the cabin. In the thick darkness, Addy knew she had heard a secret that she must keep to herself no matter how hot it burned inside her. She could feel Esther's breath on her back. Turning to face her sister, she moved close and put her arms around her. The baby's breath did not feel too warm now. Addy was glad Esther was there on the pallet with her.

As Addy fell asleep, the only voices she could hear in the night were those of the crickets in the woods.

SOLD!

Early the next morning, Addy was in the tobacco field worming the plants. She and the other children moved from row to row, carefully pulling green, wiggling worms from the leaves. The worms were as fat as her fingers, but Addy tried not to think about them. Instead, she dreamed about the kind of freedom Momma and Poppa had talked about the night before—the kind slaves ran away for. She saw herself learning to read and write. First, she'd write the names of everyone in her family. She saw herself wearing fancy dresses with lace, nothing like the rough cotton shift she always wore now. Poppa would get paid for his work and buy so much food they would never be

hungry. He would buy cloth for her fancy dresses
and Momma would make them for her.

By eleven o'clock the sun was high overhead,
and Addy felt as if she'd worked all day. She had
just finished worming her rows when it was time
for her next chore, taking water to the
field hands. The full bucket of water she
carried almost pulled her arm from her
shoulder. As Addy struggled with the
bucket, sweat ran down her dark face
and soaked the neck of her shift. But
she liked this chore because she sometimes had a
chance to see Sam or Poppa. On this day, she saw
Sam. As usual, he had a riddle for her.

"Riddle me this," said Sam. "What's smaller
than a dog but can put a bear on the run?"

Addy thought hard as Sam took the dipper from
the bucket and poured some water over his head.
From a few rows away the overseer snarled, "That
water's for drinkin', boy."

Addy saw a scowl come over Sam's face. He
mumbled, "Even a horse got to stop and cool off
sometime."

"I better get on," Addy said, worried that the

overseer might come over to them. He carried a whip.

"Naw," Sam said, his face softening. He was as tall as Poppa, but he was skinny. When he smiled, Sam still looked like a little boy. "I ain't done drinking yet, and you ain't answered my riddle. What's smaller than a dog but can put a bear on the run?" he repeated.

He took a drink while Addy thought. She looked up to see where the overseer was. He had gone off in another direction. Addy crinkled up her eyebrows and said, "A skunk?"

"You right! I don't know about you. You too smart for me, girl. Pretty soon you gonna be riddling me," Sam said.

"Real soon," said Addy, smiling at her brother.

Addy wanted to tell Sam what she had heard their parents talking about the night before. But the escape plan was so daring and dangerous, she could not share it with anyone, not even her brother. If her parents had wanted her and Sam to know, they would have told them. So Addy kept the secret inside and moved down the row to give the next field hand a drink. When the bucket was empty, she headed toward the kitchen to help Auntie Lula serve dinner to Master Stevens.

☀

The kitchen was a small brick building behind the big house. Addy hurried there, afraid she might be late. Auntie Lula was ready for Addy to work as soon as she stepped into the building. "Wash your hands good," she said, "and take that tray of food and water to the dining room."

"Yes, ma'am," Addy answered. She liked Auntie Lula. She was an old woman, old enough to be Addy's grandmother. Her skin was light and her rusty red hair was streaked with gray. She had a soft, open face, but sharp green eyes that could see right through you. Auntie Lula looked after Addy and her family. She gave them medicine when they were sick. One Christmas she had made rock candy for Addy and Sam.

The dinner Auntie Lula had cooked for Master Stevens smelled so good, Addy ached for

a bite of it. All she had had for breakfast was
cornmeal mush, and that was all she would have
for dinner. Maybe Auntie Lula would hide away
a few scraps for Addy to eat today.

Addy washed and dried her hands, and
then picked up the tray and hurried
to the dining room. Master Stevens
was sitting at the table talking
with another white man—someone
Addy had never seen before. She set
the food on the table and then poured water
for both men. As they began to eat, she took her
place standing quietly in the corner.

"You got that little girl trained real good," the
man said to Master Stevens. "She looks like a
smart one."

"I got them all trained real good," said Master
Stevens. "That's why it's such a shame to let any
of them go."

Addy's stomach turned when she heard
Master Stevens say those words. *Let any of them
go?* she thought. *What he mean, let go?*

"But I have 22 slaves to clothe and feed this
winter," Master Stevens went on, "and you know

how hard it is with the war. I need the money."

Addy stared at the floor, but she was listening very closely. She let her face go blank and empty.

"This boy you got for me," said the man, "how can I be sure he won't run on me, too? I know he's run before."

"I taught him a lesson with the whip last time he ran off," Master Stevens answered, "and you'll have his father, too. His father can control him."

They were talking about selling Sam and Poppa! Addy just knew they were. Her father had been right. Master Stevens was going to split up their family!

"Hey, girl, more water," the strange man said, turning to Addy.

Addy hurried to pour him more water.

"You sure you don't want to part with this one?" the man asked Master Stevens, patting Addy on the head.

Addy's hand shook. She wanted to pull away from his touch, to scream. But the blank look was frozen on her face. She filled the man's glass and started to pour water for Master Stevens.

"I'm not looking to sell her," Master Stevens

"You sure you don't want to part with this one?" the man asked.

replied, "but I know the price for good house servants is going up every day. Maybe when she's a little older, I'll let her go, too. By then she might fetch a price as good as her brother. She's just too young now."

Addy was listening so hard, she forgot to pay attention to her task and filled Master Stevens's glass too full. Water spilled on the table.

"See, I told you this one's too young," Master Stevens said to the man. To Addy, he said sharply, "Girl, go get a rag and clean up this mess!"

"Yes, sir," Addy said. She was glad to have a reason to run back to the kitchen. She burst through the door. "Auntie Lula," she panted. "That man fixing to take Sam and Poppa with him! Master Stevens gonna sell them!"

Auntie Lula looked worried, but when she spoke, her voice was calm.

"If that be true, we don't have much time," Auntie Lula said. "Listen to me good, now. Take your bucket and run to the well. Fill the bucket and head right to the fields where your brother and father at."

"But I already took water," Addy said.

"Hush up, child," Auntie Lula hissed. "You a smart girl. *Act* like you think it's time for the afternoon water. Walk right out to Sam and your poppa and tell them what you heard. If that man really coming for them, it's the one chance they got to run. I'll go back to the dining room. Now you get!"

Grabbing her bucket, Addy ran to the well. She ran as fast as she could, her bare feet kicking up little puffs of dust, her thick braids beating against her shoulders. *Please don't let him take Sam and Poppa. Please, God,* she prayed silently as she ran.

When Addy came to the well, she filled her bucket. She tried to run with it, but the water splashed crazily over the sides. With less than half of it left, she headed toward the fields, walking as fast as she could. Her throat was dry. *Sam! Poppa! Where you at?* she screamed inside. Outside, her eyes desperately searched the huge field.

Addy was looking for Sam and Poppa and didn't see the overseer until he stepped right into her path. "Hey, girl!" he barked at her. "What you think you doing?"

Addy was so startled, she dropped her bucket.

"I come to bring the afternoon water," she said.

"It ain't time for their afternoon water, you stupid girl. Get on out of here."

"I thought it was," Addy stammered.

"Don't give me back talk," the overseer snarled.

Addy felt frantic, but she said nothing more. She picked up her bucket and ran back to the kitchen. When she got there, she saw her mother and baby Esther with Auntie Lula. Addy rushed to Momma and threw her arms around her.

"Momma, they selling Sam and Poppa. I tried to warn them, Momma. I tried," she cried, burying her face in her mother's shoulder.

"I know you did," her mother said softly. "Auntie Lula told me."

"Master Stevens and that man headed for the barn," Auntie Lula interrupted. "Maybe they got Sam and your poppa there."

Addy's head jerked up. Maybe there was one last chance. Maybe she could still warn Sam and Poppa. Addy raced out the door and headed for the barn.

"Addy!" Momma called after her. "Wait!"

But Addy did not stop. She was not thinking,

not praying, just running, running, running. When she came to the field, she saw a wagon. Sam was in it, bound and gagged, shackled hand and foot. Master Stevens, the man from the dining room, and two other white men as big as Poppa were standing next to the wagon.

shackles

"Sam!" Addy cried out when she reached the wagon. "Oh, please, Master Stevens," Addy begged. "Don't let them take Sam."

"Get out of here, Addy," Master Stevens ordered. He had a whip in his hand.

Addy stopped where she was. Then she heard a deeper voice.

"Addy, go on now." It was her father's voice. But where was he? She looked down and then saw him lying on the ground, being chained by the overseer. Poppa's face was covered with dirt, but it was calm. She ran to him, falling on the ground next to him. "Oh, Poppa. No. No!" She threw her arms around him. He looked up at Addy.

"Everything's gonna be all right, honey. You go on," he said. There were no tears on his face, but Addy knew he was crying inside.

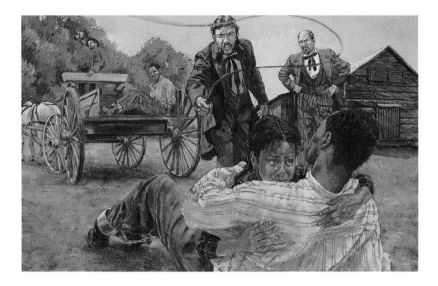

"Get back, girl," Master Stevens barked. Addy heard his whip crack. She felt a lash of fire on her back as if she had been burned. But still she held on to Poppa.

Master Stevens growled at her. "I told you to get. Now get before I whip you again." He reached for Addy and yanked her away from Poppa.

Addy fell backward into her mother's arms. Momma held Addy close, both of them crying. This time, even Momma couldn't keep the pain hidden inside.

A NEW PLAN

 It was late on Friday afternoon, nearly a week after Sam and Poppa had been sold. Addy and the other children were worming tobacco plants. They were to work their way down the long rows, turning over every leaf to find the worms and kill them. It was a job Addy hated. She didn't even like looking at the worms. To kill them, she had to either squish them with her hands or squash them under her bare feet.

Addy's mind was not on her work. All her thoughts were about Poppa and Sam. *Hey, I got a riddle for you, Sam*, she thought to herself. *What's heavy as a full pail of water, but still empty, empty, empty? Give up? It's my heart.* She peeled the worms off some plants but forgot to look under the leaves of others. When she came to the end of her second row, the overseer came along behind her to check her work.

Addy was just starting the next row when she saw the overseer storming toward her. He had his whip in one hand. She turned to run, but he got to her before she could take a step. Addy raised up her hands, thinking he was going to hit her.

But he did not hit her. He dropped the whip and pulled Addy's hands down from her face, yanking her toward him. Holding her wrists in one of his large hands, he opened his other hand. Addy saw what he held—live worms. Worms that Addy had missed. The overseer forced open her mouth and stuffed the still-twisting and wiggling worms inside.

Addy began choking.

"Eat them!" the overseer growled. "Chew them up—every last one of them. If you don't, I'll get some more."

Addy gagged as the worms' juicy bodies burst in her mouth.

"That'll teach you to mind your work," the

overseer snapped. He shoved her away. Addy crumpled to the ground as he turned to leave.

☀

It was dark when Momma came home to the cabin that night. She had baby Esther on her hip. There was no fire in the hearth. Addy lay curled up on her pallet. Her face, arms, and legs were streaked with dirt. Her feet were covered with mud.

"Addy, you awake? Get up, honey," her mother said, lighting a candle and then placing Esther down on the pallet. But Addy did not even look up.

"Addy," her mother said in a voice as soft and warm as the glow of the candle. "What happened to you?" She sat down on the edge of Addy's pallet and touched her head gently.

Addy opened her eyes. They were red. As she told her mother about what the overseer had done to her, she started to cry. Momma lifted Addy's head onto her lap. "I hate them, Momma. I hate white people," Addy sobbed.

"I don't want you to hate nobody," Momma

said, stroking Addy's hair. After a while, she got up to get some water. When she came back, she began washing the tears and dirt from Addy's face.

"Don't you hate them, Momma?" Addy asked.

"No, I don't hate white people," Momma answered. "Honey, if you fill your heart with hate, there ain't gonna be no room for love. Your brother and Poppa need us to fill our hearts with love for them, not hate for white people."

"But Momma, that overseer and Master Stevens, they hate us," Addy said bitterly. "Why white people hate us and treat us wrong?"

"Addy, all white people don't hate colored people. Not all of them do us bad. Master Stevens was wrong to sell Sam and Poppa and to whip you. But Addy, people can do wrong for such a long time, they don't even know it's wrong no more. What's worse is when people hurt each other and don't even care they hurting them. Like that overseer. He a mean man. That's what hate do to people. I don't want you to ever be that kind of person."

Esther began crying. Addy reached over and handed her rag doll to the baby. Esther quieted down.

"Addy, there something I need to talk to you about," Momma said slowly, "something serious. You listening to me? Your poppa and me talked about something before Master Stevens sold him and Sam. Poppa was worried about the war, and times getting hard . . ."

Addy knew what her mother was going to say. With all that had happened in the past week, Addy had almost forgotten about the secret she had been keeping, but now she let it out. "You and Poppa planned for us all to run away," she said.

"How did you know that?" Momma asked.

"I heard y'all talking one night," Addy answered. "I didn't mean to listen, but I couldn't help it."

"Then you already know we planned to go north," said Momma. "Well, we still going."

"What about Poppa and Sam?" Addy asked. "Shouldn't we wait for them to come back for us?"

"They ain't coming back here ever again, no matter what," Momma replied. "Poppa's plan was to go to Philadelphia. He told Sam about it the day after you heard us talking. I aim to stick to that plan, and we leaving tomorrow night."

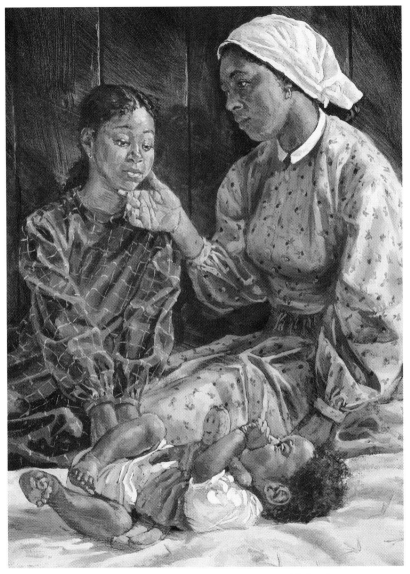

"Addy, I need to talk to you," Momma said slowly.

Addy looked into her mother's thin face. There were fine lines of worry around her brown eyes.

"Tomorrow! But what if we get caught?" Addy asked, her voice shaking.

"There ain't no choice, honey. I never thought Master Stevens would break up our family after your poppa and me served him our whole life. But I was wrong." Momma shook her head. "After what he done, Addy, I can't keep you safe here no more. I'm scared that man who bought Sam and your poppa might come back for you. I can't stop him if he do. I ain't gonna sit here and wait for him or anybody to come take you from me."

Esther started to cry again, and Addy patted her gently. Then she said, "Momma, I'm scared, but I want to go to freedom. Esther want to go, too." She turned to her baby sister. "Don't you want to go to freedom, Esther?" Addy asked. "Don't you want to go find Poppa and Sam in Philadelphia?"

"Addy, go to my pallet and get what's under it," Momma said.

Under Momma's pallet were two large kerchiefs and some clothes. They were not clothes for a woman and a girl, but for a man and a boy.

"Momma, what we gonna do with these?" asked Addy.

"I'm gonna pack them kerchiefs with some food, a drinking gourd, things like that. We wearing the clothes," answered Momma.

kerchiefs and drinking gourd

"We gonna be disguised?" asked Addy in surprise.

"They a disguise, but they more than that," explained Momma. "Auntie Lula and Uncle Solomon got them for us. When Master Stevens send out his dogs after us, it's gonna be hard for them to track our smell if we got on somebody else's clothes."

"Auntie Lula and Uncle Solomon should come with us, Momma," said Addy. "Poppa say Uncle Solomon know where the safe house is. They should come to freedom, too."

"They too old to come to freedom, Addy. They can't run," Momma said. "They would slow us down."

"Esther can't run neither, and she coming," Addy said.

Momma lowered her head. Addy knew something was wrong. Her mother would not look at her. Then Addy saw tears on her mother's face.

"Momma, what's the matter?" Addy asked.

"I may as well tell you now, honey," her mother said, her voice slow and sad. "Esther ain't coming with us."

Addy could not believe her ears. She must not have heard right. She picked up Esther and held her close.

"No, Momma," Addy said. "We ain't leaving Esther."

"Addy, did you hear me?" Momma's voice was soft but firm. "Your sister is staying here."

"But why? Poppa said we was all going," Addy insisted.

"Honey, it was different when your poppa and Sam was going with us. They could help carry Esther. Now I got to carry her by myself."

"I could help, Momma. Let me help. I could carry her," Addy begged.

"Besides," Momma went on, "Esther might cry any time. Her crying would give us away."

"I could keep her quiet, Momma, I just know I

could," Addy said. "I'd let her hold Janie while we was running."

"Addy, Esther can't come," her mother said.

Addy hugged Esther again.

"This the hardest thing I ever had to do in my life," Momma went on. "I love Esther as much as I love you and Sam, but we can't take her. Auntie Lula and Uncle Solomon is gonna keep her. She just a baby, so Master Stevens ain't gonna sell her. He can't make no money selling a baby."

Addy cradled Esther in her arms, gently rocking her back and forth. The three of them sat quietly for a long time. Then Momma broke the silence. "The war ain't gonna last forever. When it's over, we gonna get Esther back. Our family will be together again. Lay down now," Momma said, blowing out the candle.

"Momma, can we all sleep together tonight?" Addy asked.

"I'd like that," Momma said.

Addy, Momma, and Esther crowded onto Addy's pallet. Esther was sandwiched between Addy and Momma. The baby held tight to Janie.

Addy moved as close to Esther as she could to

feel the baby's warm breath on her face. She put her arms around her tiny sister. Addy tried not to cry, but itchy, hot tears were running down her face, and she didn't bother brushing them away. She felt her mother's arms around both her and the baby. Beyond, from the deeper darkness of the woods, Addy heard a single owl hooting in the night.

CHAPTER
FOUR

—

INTO THE NIGHT

The next night, after it was fully dark, with not a streak of orange or red in the sky, Auntie Lula and Uncle Solomon came to Addy's cabin. Addy and her mother were in their disguises, with their kerchiefs packed. The well-worn clothes were baggy on them. Esther was sleeping on Addy's pallet.

Uncle Solomon had two hats with him. One was a straw hat that he gave Addy's mother. The other, a felt hat, he placed on Addy's head.

"Now, there's magic in your hat," Uncle Solomon said to Addy, trying to cheer her up. Addy did not feel like smiling.

"Don't you believe that hat got magic?" Uncle

33

Solomon asked. He snapped his fingers near her left ear. "Why, look what's come out your ear. You

must've forgot to wash behind it. Look at this half dime I found there." He handed the coin to Addy.

Addy reached behind her ear. "How'd you do that?" she asked.

"Shhh," Uncle Solomon said. "It's magic. You hold on to that half dime. You gonna need it where you going. Freedom cost, you hear me? Freedom's got its cost."

"Come on, Solomon, they ain't got all night," Auntie Lula said. "Look here, I got some food and things for you," she said, handing Addy's mother a small sack.

Addy's mother put the sack into her kerchief, and then she bent down to pick up Esther. Esther woke and began to fuss.

Addy watched Momma as she hugged the baby hard and kissed her over and over. She searched Momma's face for tears, but there weren't any, not on the outside at least. Addy kissed Esther, too, and stroked her head. "Don't worry, Esther. We coming back for you," she whispered softly as she handed

her rag doll to the baby. "You hold on to Janie until I see you again," Addy said. Then her mother gave Esther to Auntie Lula.

"We gonna take good care of Esther. Don't worry," Auntie Lula said, looking into the baby's eyes as she held her. "She gonna be right here when you come back for her."

Uncle Solomon gave Addy and Momma some final advice. "Go fast as you can at night and hide during the day. Every time you see water, go through it. A creek, a river—I don't care if it ain't nothing but a puddle, go through it. That way you

won't hardly leave no scent for the dogs to pick up
on. And watch out for them Confederate soldiers.
They dressed up in gray uniforms. They can be
mean as snakes, and if they catch you, they gonna
bring you back to slavery."

"God be with you," Auntie Lula said as Addy
and her mother turned to leave the little cabin.
Esther began to cry as they slipped out into the
damp, warm night and ran into the woods. Addy
looked back to catch a final glimpse of her baby
sister, but tears blurred her sight.

※

The full moon shone in the eastern
sky, looking like a half dime shining
in the bottom of a well. At first, the
moonlight shone through the tall pines,
filling the forest with a silver light. Addy and her
mother ran from shadow to shadow like a deer
with her fawn. But as they moved deeper into the
woods, only a small glimmer of moonlight made its
way through the thick branches of the trees. There
were dark, eerie shadows everywhere, and it was
hard to see. Momma took Addy's hand as they

hurried along, stumbling over vines and stumps hidden by the darkness.

Addy expected to hear the comforting night sound of the crickets that she always heard at the cabin, but the deeper they got in the woods, the stranger the sounds became. Owls screeched high in the pines. The wind moaned like a wounded animal. Branches from saplings reached out for her, stinging her face as they slapped against her. A bat swooped down from the trees, its wings beating the air just above their heads. Suddenly a dark form stirred in the bushes ahead, moving toward them. Addy screamed and froze. Momma jerked to a stop and clamped her hand over Addy's mouth.

"Hush up," her mother whispered sharply. "You can't holler out."

The bushes moved again. Addy's heart beat very fast. Bump-bump-bump-bump. Bump-bump-bump-bump.

Slowly, Momma took her hand away from Addy's mouth. "It's only a possum or a skunk," she said calmly.

Addy let out a sigh of relief. "Momma, I ain't mean to holler," she whispered. "We left Esther behind because her crying might give us away. But I hollered louder than Esther ever could." Addy remembered what her father had said about not always showing your feelings. She would have to learn to keep them inside sometimes.

All through the night, Addy and Momma stumbled through the darkness. They waded through swampy places where their feet were sucked deep into oozing mud. They clawed through prickly vines. The thorns snatched at their clothes and dug into Addy's hands until they bled. Bare roots tore through the tough skin on the soles of Addy's feet. Once she stubbed her toe on a rock and fell down. But this time Addy did not cry out. All night long, she and Momma pushed on and on.

Just when Addy thought she could not go another step, the sky began to lighten. She could see Momma's face for the first time in hours. It was streaked with dirt. She touched her own face and felt dried blood on her cheek from a cut below her eye.

"We better stop soon, Momma," Addy said

softly. "It's getting light out and somebody might see us."

"You right," Momma said. "We need to look for a hiding place."

They went a little farther and found a small cave. They crawled inside and huddled together, waiting for sleep to come.

When they woke up hours later, it was hot. Mosquitoes buzzed around their heads, drawn to the stickiness of their sweaty skin. Addy slapped at them, but it was no use.

"You must be hungry," Momma said, reaching into her bundle. She handed Addy a piece of Auntie Lula's cornbread. It was hard and dry, but it tasted good to Addy. She washed it down with a drink of water from the gourd.

When they finished eating, Momma reached into the bundle again. "I got something for you," she said. Addy watched eagerly as Momma opened her hand. In her palm was a small, shiny shell.

"I want you to have this," Momma said. "It's something me and your poppa been saving for you. This cowrie shell belonged to Poppa's grandma. She was stole from Africa when she was no bigger than you. None of her family was on the ship with her when she came here from across the water. She wore this shell on a necklace. Your poppa was gonna give it to you when you was older, but I think you should have it now, Addy. Your great-grandma's name was *Aduke*. That name got a meaning where she come from. It means 'much loved.' I saved her name for you, Addy."

Addy was silent for a moment. Then she looked into her mother's gentle brown eyes. "Momma, can I hold the shell tonight?"

"Sure you can. I got something special to put it on," her mother said, pulling a leather string out of her bundle.

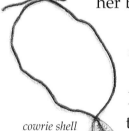

cowrie shell

"Momma, that's one of Sam's shoelaces," Addy said.

"I wanted you to have something of his, too," her mother said. She pulled the cord through a small hole in one end of the shell, knotted it, and then put it around Addy's neck. "Remember what I told you about the love you need to carry in your heart. It ain't nothing you can touch like this shell, but when you find yourself feeling sad or scared, you dip into that love, Addy. It's a well with no bottom, and it can give you strength and courage."

Addy rubbed the shell between her fingers. Its rounded top was smooth as soap. The flat underside was also smooth, except for the middle where the shell closed in on itself. There it felt like the teeth of a fine comb.

"My great-grandma must have been brave to come across the water all alone. I'm gonna be brave just like she was," Addy said.

"She *was* brave, Addy," Momma answered, "and you brave, too. But there's one thing different about you and your great-grandma. Her journey ended in slavery. Yours, girl, is taking you to freedom."

They sat in silence a long time, looking at the cowrie shell and thinking about someone they had never met.

Then Addy spoke. "Momma, do you think Esther gonna remember us?"

"That ain't easy to say. Babies don't remember much, but I got a feeling Auntie Lula won't let her forget," Momma said.

As Addy and Momma settled down in the cave to wait for sunset, Addy pictured Esther back on the plantation. She would be asleep now, curled up with Janie. Maybe she would be thinking about Addy.

☀

When night finally came, Addy and Momma started out again. The moon lit their way until they reached the end of the woods, where they saw a flat darkness ahead of them. Then, before they could see water, they heard the rushing sound of it. They had come to a wide river.

"This got to be the river near the Gifford plantation that Poppa talked about," Addy whispered.

"We got to cross it," Momma said, her voice sounding scared. "We better stuff our hats and things in our pockets."

They stood on the bank of the river for a few moments, afraid to enter the foaming, angry water. Sam had taught Addy how to swim, but this water looked dangerous—and Momma didn't know how to swim at all.

Holding tight to each other, they started into the water together. Addy picked her way along the squishy bottom, her feet slipping on the slimy rocks that were stuck in the mud. Once she tripped on a rock, losing her balance and pulling Momma with her. Addy felt her mother's grip tighten around her hand and realized again how frightened Momma was.

Pulling themselves up, they slowly made their way to the center of the river. There the current started to pull at them. It lifted them off the bottom and dragged them sideways. Hard as they tried to walk against it, the water was stronger than they were, and they were pushed farther and farther away from shore. Addy could hear Momma sputter as water filled her mouth and nose.

"Momma, keep your head up," Addy yelled as loud as she dared. "Just don't go under."

Suddenly a huge swell of water rushed against them, pulling Momma's hand from Addy's, dragging her away. Addy turned just in time to see her mother disappear beneath the churning water.

Addy wanted to scream, but she kept it inside. Instead, she drew in air, filling her lungs, and dove

Addy turned just in time to see her mother disappear beneath the water.

under the water. She struggled against the current, trying to stay close to the place where Momma had disappeared. She couldn't see a thing in the dark water. She felt around for Momma, but she found nothing. Addy's lungs began to burn. She was running out of air. Popping up above the water, she looked around frantically.

"Momma," she called, gulping for air. "Momma, where you at?"

Afraid no answer would come, she dove down again. This time she let the current push her while she dragged her arms through the water, searching for her mother. Suddenly, Addy was stopped by a fallen tree under the water. She groped among the branches, but their sharp ends jabbed and poked her. She kicked furiously to get away when suddenly her foot hit something soft. It was Momma, trapped in the branches. Addy braced herself against a large limb, grabbed Momma, and then pushed off against the tree with all her strength to bring both of them to the surface.

Gasping for air, the two struggled to the far shore. Clutching each other, they finally reached the shallows where the water calmed. Exhausted and breathless, they fell on the riverbank. When Addy could finally talk, she whispered, "Momma, is you all right?"

"You saved me, Addy," Momma said weakly. "You a brave girl."

Addy was shivering as she and her mother got up and slowly made their way into the woods. Their wet clothes stuck to them. Momma had lost her kerchief, and her hat was ripped. Addy pulled her own hat from her pocket. Other than being wet, it looked fine. She pulled it down tight on her head and thought, *Maybe it is a lucky hat.*

She reached to see if the cowrie shell was still around her neck. It was there, and something else was, too. It felt like a wet leaf. When she peeled it off, Addy realized it was a leech. She shuddered and quietly flicked it away.

leech

☀

Addy and her mother traveled for hours before Momma spotted the railroad tracks. Addy had never seen tracks before. They were shining silver, and they pointed the way north to freedom.

"These got to be the tracks your father talked

about," Momma whispered. "We got to be extra careful out here. There ain't hardly a place to hide."

They had seen no one since they started their escape, but tracks meant a train could come at any time. Travelers might spot them. They could trust no one.

Addy and her mother followed the path of the tracks in the moonlight. When the noises of the night were gone and birdsongs began to fill the air, they found a thick clump of pine trees near a curve in the tracks. Gathering dead branches and brush, they made a shelter and crawled inside.

Addy could barely keep her eyes open. She was too tired to slap at the ants that crawled on her legs or swat at the flies buzzing over her head. She curled up and rested her head on her mother's chest.

"I'm real proud of you," Momma whispered as she gently stroked Addy's hair away from her face. Addy smiled. She could feel her mother's heart beating. It was a soothing sound.

CHAPTER
FIVE
—

FREEDOM TAKEN

A low rumble woke Addy and her mother. Addy thought it sounded like thunder. Then a light appeared far in the distance. Addy could see it moving toward her, getting bigger and bigger. It looked as if the moon had fallen from the sky and was rolling through the tops of the trees. Safe in the darkness, Addy and her mother crept out of their shelter just in time to see something Addy had only heard about. A train!

She could make out its shape charging through the darkness. The engine was spitting red sparks, and a ribbon of smoke ran along the length of the train. As it passed along a curve in the tracks, Addy watched its rear light disappear into the distance. But instead of moving away in a straight line, the train turned to the right. Addy was puzzled. Then she understood—the train had turned onto a set of tracks she could not even see yet.

"Momma, we here!" Addy said, a little too loudly. She lowered her voice. "The safe house has to be near the place where the train turned! We did it. We made it, Momma!" Addy threw her arms around Momma.

"I think you right," Momma said. "Let's go."

Addy and her mother ran hand in hand toward the place where the train had turned.

"We safe now," Addy exclaimed. "We going to Philadelphia."

"We ain't there yet," Momma said sharply. "Hush, now."

"We gonna see Sam and Poppa," Addy went on. "Then we come back for Esther, and the whole family be together again." Addy pictured them all in Philadelphia, living in a beautiful house.

"Freedom ain't that easy, girl," warned Momma. "Don't get your hopes too high."

But Addy didn't hear her. Spurred on by her

thoughts of Philadelphia, she moved faster and faster, pulling away from Momma. Running fast, she felt the cowrie shell beat against her chest. She was going to freedom.

It was a long way to the place where the train had turned, but Addy was still running when she saw a small light. It looked like the glow of a lantern. Addy thought it must be in the window of the safe house. She raced toward it, her mother far behind. It was not until she was closer that she saw she was wrong. She stopped suddenly. The light was from a small campfire in a clearing near the tracks. A group of men were gathered around it. Addy could see them lying on the ground, sleeping. She was about to turn and run back the other way when she heard a gruff voice call out, "Who's there?"

Addy turned. She could see the face of a white man in the light of the fire. He had on a gray jacket and gray hat. He was a Confederate soldier, and he was staring right at her!

"Oh, it's you, boy. Bring me some water," the soldier said.

Although Addy knew he was looking right at

Addy heard a gruff voice call out, "Who's there?"

her, she didn't think he was talking to her. He was talking to some boy. But what boy? Just then Addy remembered the disguise. *She* was the boy!

Desperately, Addy looked around. Then she saw a bucket of water. To get to it she had to walk right through the soldiers' camp. She saw another soldier on the ground stir. He rolled over. What if they all woke up and captured her?

Addy lowered her head, touched the cowrie shell briefly, and began to move. Inside she was shaking, but on the outside she was walking straight and strong past the sleeping soldiers. She picked up the bucket and brought it to the soldier.

"Train scare you, did it, boy?" the soldier asked.

Addy kept her head down and nodded.

"You'll get used to it after a while. Get on back to sleep," the soldier said.

Addy wanted to rush back into the woods, but she knew she couldn't. She acted as though she belonged in the camp. She walked to the edge of the clearing and lay down. The soldier lay down, too, and Addy waited a few minutes until she could hear him snoring. Then, as quietly as she could, Addy crept away from the soldiers and into the woods. *I got to warn Momma,* Addy thought. Just when she had gotten far enough away from the camp to start running, someone reached out and grabbed her.

It was Momma. She pulled Addy so close to her that Addy could feel the shell pressed between them. Momma held Addy for a long moment and then led her away.

When they were far from the camp, Momma spoke at last. "I was watching you with them soldiers, Addy, and I was holding my breath the whole time. But you did it, girl. You kept your feelings inside this time. Your poppa would be proud of you."

They walked farther along the tracks until they came to the place where two sets of tracks met and formed a silvery cross. A house stood just beyond the cross up on a little hill. It was white with red shutters. Poppa had been right.

To Addy it seemed that the house was just waiting for them. They did not have to run to it. They only had to walk and knock on the door where freedom was. It would open to them.

Addy and her mother crouched in the shadows, staring at the white house. There was no light from inside.

"Why we waiting?" Addy whispered.

"I don't know if it's safe," her mother said. "There might be more of them soldiers around."

"It's got to be safe," Addy said. "It's a safe house."

"Addy, it ain't that simple," Momma said. "Your poppa said a white woman live there. Them soldiers might be coming in and out of there. I don't trust them."

"But Momma, we got to trust the white woman. If we don't, where we gonna go?" Addy asked.

Without answering, Momma took a deep breath and stood, pulling Addy up with her. They slipped out of the shadows and walked to the house.

Momma tapped lightly on the door. No answer came. She tapped again, and still there was no answer.

Addy looked at her mother's face. It was calm

and still. At last, a light glowed in the house. Through a small window, Addy could see the light of a candle move through the dark house. She heard the door being unlatched on the other side.

It opened, and an old woman not much taller than Addy stood before them. Her face shone in the light of her candle.

"Miss Caroline? Can you help us?" Addy asked.

Addy saw the woman's face twist into an angry scowl. "I thought I told you not to come here, boy. Go back and tell those soldiers I won't help them," Miss Caroline said. She started to shut the door.

Addy stuck her foot in the door to keep it from closing. "We ain't with them soldiers, ma'am," Addy said quickly, "and I ain't no boy." Addy pulled her hat off, revealing her braids. "Me and my momma running away to freedom. Can you help us?"

Addy saw the look on the woman's face soften. All the anger washed from it.

"Come in," Miss Caroline said. "Please come in."

Addy and her mother stepped inside. The woman quickly closed the door behind them and led them to the kitchen.

"My, oh my," Miss Caroline said. "Those are some fine disguises. I thought you were with those Confederate soldiers. They got here yesterday and sent a boy right over here to ask me for food. But I didn't give them one crumb. I don't cotton to those Rebels. You must be tired and hungry. I don't have much, and nothing fancy. But you're welcome to it. Sit down and I'll start a fire."

Addy and her mother sat watching the woman work. She seemed to be everywhere, starting the fire, dragging a tin tub next to it, heating a large pot of water, putting plates on the small table.

"Let us help," Momma said.

"No, you sit and rest. I know you must be tired," Miss Caroline said. "Who sent you here?"

"Uncle Solomon," Addy's mother said. "We trying to get to Philadelphia."

"Oh, Solomon," the woman sighed. "I've known him for over fifty years—since we were both children on farms that were next to each other." She served Addy and her mother some rice and boiled greens. Addy felt safe in this small, warm home. While Addy and Momma ate, Miss Caroline left the kitchen. When she returned, she had a bundle of clothes in her arms.

"These are clothes I save for runaways. After your bath, you find something that fits. You can rest here tonight. Then I'll take you to the coast. You can get a ship to Philadelphia from there. We have to leave before sunup—before those soldiers wake in the morning and come back here."

"Thank you so much, ma'am," Addy's mother said. "I wish I could do something for you."

Addy went to her bundle and untied it. She took out the half dime Uncle Solomon had given her and held it out to the woman.

"Oh, I don't want money," Miss Caroline said, "and I don't want you to do anything for me. There's no need to thank me. You both are so brave to have escaped and come so far. It's thanks enough to know I'm helping you have a new life."

Addy and her mother took long, hot baths. The dirt from their journey melted off them in the warm water. That night, for the first time in their lives, Addy and Momma slept on a real mattress, not one full of itchy cornhusks. Addy tried to stay awake so she could think about how good it felt to be clean and safe, but she was too tired. She fell asleep in Momma's arms.

Before the sun came up, Addy, Momma, and Miss Caroline got ready to leave the small white house with the red shutters. Momma was dressed in a brown dress, Addy in a pink one.

Addy loved her dress with its wiggly white stripes and white buttons running down the front. It was prettier than any she had imagined when she dreamed about freedom.

Miss Caroline had found a pair of drawers and a straw bonnet that just fit Addy. After Addy tied the ribbon of the hat under her chin, she stood straight and tall for her mother to see.

"How I look, Momma?" Addy asked.

Momma's eyes filled with tears. "I wish your poppa could see you now, child."

Outside, Miss Caroline hid Addy and her mother in the back of her wagon and covered them with some old sacks. The wagon rocked gently as it pulled away from the safe house. Addy lay close to her mother. She reached to her neck and felt for the shell. Holding it tightly, Addy thought of Esther, Sam, Poppa, and even her great-grandma who had come across the water alone. They were with her, all of them. With the deep well of love in her heart, she could feel them with her.

"Momma, we done it," Addy said softly. "Just like Poppa said. We took our freedom."

LOOKING
BACK
1864

A Peek Into
the Past

Newly freed African Americans in 1862

More than 300 years before Addy was born, the first black people arrived in North America from Africa. Some African Americans were explorers and pioneers who came with hope and determination to start a new life. But most blacks came as slaves, brought to America on ships by slave traders. The traders had captured or bought them in Africa, taking them from

Phillis Wheatley wrote poetry in the 1770s, a time when most Americans couldn't read.

A group of captive Africans on their way to a slave ship

In 1791 Benjamin Banneker helped plan the city of Washington, D.C., our nation's capital.

62

Some slaves were trained as carpenters and made fine furniture like this cabinet.

their families, their tribes, and their homeland. In Africa they had a life that was rich in art, religion, music, and language. But in America they were forced to work against their will, without pay, for life.

By Addy's time, most slaves worked on *plantations,* or large farms, in the southern part of the United States. Plantation owners in the South depended on slaves to tend their crops because that was a cheap way to get the work done. Most plantation slaves were field hands who planted, tended, and harvested crops, but some slaves were blacksmiths, shoemakers, and carpenters. Some enslaved people worked in their owners' houses as cooks, nursemaids, and seamstresses.

Some house slaves cared for their owners' children.

Field slaves at work on a cotton plantation

Slaves were sometimes shackled in leg irons as punishment.

The treatment of slaves varied widely, but owners usually provided just enough food and clothing for slaves to survive. Most slaves lived on their owners' plantations in one-room cabins with dirt floors and a few pieces of poor furniture. House slaves had better food and clothing than those who worked in the fields, but they often had to live in their owners' homes, apart from their families. Owners might punish their slaves by making them eat tobacco worms, just as Addy had to. They might whip their slaves or shackle their feet or hands so they couldn't move. Worst of all, owners could divide up and sell slave families, as Addy's owner did.

A row of slave cabins

Enslaved people maintained strong family ties when they were allowed to live together, and even when their families were broken up. They did this by extending their families to include people they were not related to—slaves who

Four generations of a slave family in 1862

were new to a plantation or left behind when their family members were sold.

Slaves developed their own art, music, religious beliefs, and stories based on African traditions. They passed along to their children stories, names, and knowledge from Africa. For example, Addy's whole name, *Aduke*, came from Yoruba, one of the languages of West Africa. Words we still use today—like *yam, canoe,* and *banjo*— come from various West African languages.

Slave parents made simple dolls and other toys for their children.

Legally, slaves could gather in groups only if a white person was present.

Spirituals are religious folk songs created by slaves based on African music styles. Spirituals expressed the singers' suffering and protest, and their hope for freedom. Slaves also sang spirituals to send secret messages to each other that the slave owner wouldn't understand. For instance, slaves might sing "Steal away, steal away, steal away to Jesus" to spread news of plans to escape. Spirituals remain popular today. Jazz also grew out of African rhythms. It is the only kind of music originally created in the United States.

Slaves enjoyed making music with handmade instruments like this gourd fiddle.

A Virginia slave named Nat Turner and several followers led a revolt against slavery in 1831.

Slaves opposed their treatment in many ways. They worked very slowly on purpose, burned crops, pretended to be sick, tried to earn money to buy their freedom, and asked the courts to set them free. By the early 1800s, most northern states had made slavery illegal. And in 1808, it became illegal to bring slaves into the United States. But the buying and selling of slaves continued in the South for more than 50 years, until Addy's time.

Signs like this one advertised the sale of slaves.

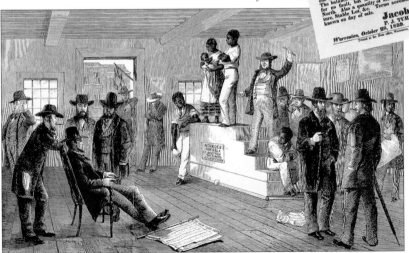

A family of slaves being sold at an auction

The Civil War put an end to the Underground Railroad, but many slaves still made dangerous attempts to escape to freedom.

Harriet Tubman escaped slavery and helped over 300 runaway slaves gain freedom.

Frederick Douglass was an abolitionist leader.

People who were against slavery were called *abolitionists*. As slavery grew in the South, more and more people, especially in the North, became abolitionists. Abolitionists, both black and white, helped slaves escape on the Underground Railroad. The Underground Railroad wasn't a real railroad. It was a series of routes and hiding "stations" leading north to freedom. Escaping slaves traveled at night, hidden by darkness, usually to the northern states or Canada. Harriet Tubman, an escaped slave herself, secretly returned to the South 19 times to guide others to freedom. Escaping required great courage, because runaway slaves who were caught were brutally punished.

The man in the center escaped slavery by hiding in a box while it was shipped to the North.

Eleven southern states left the Union to form the Confederate States of America.

When Addy and her mother escaped, northern states were fighting against southern states in the Civil War. This war had many causes, but one of the most important was the disagreement about slavery. People in the North felt slavery should not be legal. In 1861, several southern states _seceded_, or separated, from the United States. These states formed their own nation, called the Confederate States of America. President Abraham Lincoln believed it was wrong for the southern states to secede, and he eventually declared war against the South. That war was called the War Between the States, or the Civil War.

In the beginning, Lincoln declared war to keep all the states in the nation together, not to end slavery. But later, on January 1,

Union and Confederate soldiers in a battle of the Civil War

1863, Lincoln proclaimed that all slaves in those states still fighting the North were _emancipated_, or free. Because the South had decided that it was a separate nation, it ignored the Emancipation Proclamation. That's why many people, like Addy's family, were still risking their lives to escape slavery in 1864.

MORE TO DISCOVER!

While books are the heart of The American Girls Collection,® they are only the beginning. The stories in the Collection come to life when you act them out with the beautiful American Girls dolls and their exquisite clothes and accessories. To request a free catalogue full of things girls love, send in this postcard, call **1-800-845-0005,** or visit our Web site at **americangirl.com**.

Please send me an American Girl® catalogue.

My name is _____

My address is _____

City _____ State _____ Zip _____

My birth date is ____ / ____ / ____ E-mail address _____
    month   day   year

Parent's signature _____

And send a catalogue to my friend:

My friend's name is _____

Address _____

City _____ State _____ Zip _____

If the postcard has already been removed from this book
and you would like to receive an American Girl® catalogue,
please send your name and address to:

American Girl
P.O. Box 620497
Middleton, WI 53562-0497

You may also call our toll-free number, **1-800-845-0005,**
or visit our Web site at **americangirl.com**.

Place
Stamp
Here

PO BOX 620497
MIDDLETON WI 53562-0497